The Skunk

Story by

Mac Barnett

Art by

Patrick McDonnell

ROARING BROOK PRESS
NEW YORK

This one's for Paul Saint-Amour

—M.B.

Published by Roaring Brook Press
Roaring Brook Press is a division of Holtzbrinck Publishing Holdings Limited Partnership
175 Fifth Avenue, New York, New York 10010
mackids.com

Library of Congress Cataloging-in-Publication Data

Barnett, Mac.
The skunk / Mac Barnett ; illustrated by Patrick McDonnell.
    pages cm
 Summary: "A man is followed by a skunk all day until the tables turn"—
Provided by publisher.
 ISBN 978-1-59643-966-5 (hardback)
[1. Skunks—Fiction. 2. Human-animal relationships—Fiction. 3. Humorous
stories.] I. McDonnell, Patrick, 1956– illustrator. II. Title.
 PZ7.B26615Sku 2015
 [E]—dc23
                                                          2014032753

Roaring Brook Press books may be purchased for business or promotional use.
For information on bulk purchases please contact Macmillan Corporate and Premium
Sales Department at (800) 221-7945 x5442 or by email at specialmarkets@macmillan.com.

First edition 2015
Book design by Jeff Schulz
Printed in China by RR Donnelley Asia Printing Solutions Ltd., Dongguan City, Guangdong Province
10 9 8 7 6

When I left my house
there was a skunk on my doorstep.

I kept very still. I did not want to startle him.
But the skunk did not seem scared.

Slowly and carefully, I backed away
and started down the street.

The skunk started right after me.

We walked together a few blocks.
I thought it was funny that a skunk
and I could be going in the same direction.

But after a mile I realized
I was being followed.

When I sped up, the skunk sped up.

When I slowed, the skunk slowed.

I took many wild turns.

And so did the skunk.

I turned to the skunk.
I asked, "What do you want?"

The skunk did not answer.
The skunk was a skunk.

I bought the skunk an apple.
I gave him a saucer of milk.
I offered him my pocket watch.

The skunk did not want
any of these things.

This was ridiculous.
I was wasting my time.
I hailed a taxi and sped off
down the avenue.

The skunk took the next cab.

Outside the opera house, I hid behind a shrub.

The skunk did not see me crouching there.

Success! I bounded up the steps and took my seat.
I was relieved to find myself between a lady
and a gray old officer. But then of course
skunks can't buy tickets to the opera!

The curtain rose, and I smiled.

In the middle of the first solo,
the skunk came trotting down the aisle.

He climbed up the lady's gown
and took a seat on her head.
She did not notice. She was rapt.

"Excuse me, madam," I said,
"but there seems to be a skunk on your head."

"Hush," said the lady.
"This is my favorite part. So strange and so sad."

I had to escape!
I excused myself and hurried out a fire exit.

The skunk pursued me across the city.
He followed me through the
sculpture garden and the cemetery.
I could not get away!

I ran to the carnival and bought a ticket to
the Ferris wheel. The skunk boarded the gondola
after mine. We rode around in great circles.
He was not getting any nearer,
but he was not getting farther away.

I'll admit that I began to panic.
I ran past the wharf and turned down an alley.
It was a dead end.

The skunk walked toward me.
"Go away, skunk!" I shouted.
But the skunk came closer and closer.

I lifted a manhole and
climbed down into the sewers.

I hurried underneath the streets.
Many times I paused to catch my breath,
but never for long. I had to go on.

When I came up,
I was in a different part of the city.

I found a new house.
I bought new things.

And on my first night,
when I opened my bedroom door,

guess who was waiting there for me?

Nobody.

I threw myself a party.
I cooked a large dinner.
People brought me gifts.

After dessert, during the dancing,

I thought about the skunk.

What was he doing?
Was he looking for me?

Was he back in his burrow?
Was he following someone else?

I left the party to find my skunk.

He was not in the alley.

He was not in
the carnival.

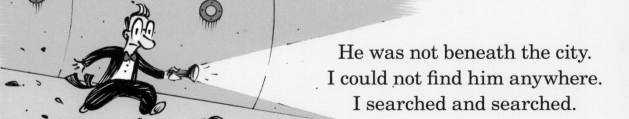

He was not beneath the city.
I could not find him anywhere.
I searched and searched.

There was the skunk!

I trailed him down the sidewalk,
careful to remain hidden.

I think I will keep an eye on him
and make sure he does not follow me again.